## Put Beginning Readers on the Right Track with
## ALL ABOARD READING™

The All Aboard Reading series is especially for beginning readers. Written by noted authors and illustrated in full color, these are books that children really and truly *want* to read—books to excite their imagination, tickle their funny bone, expand their interests, and support their feelings. With four different reading levels, All Aboard Reading lets you choose which books are most appropriate for your children and their growing abilities.

### Picture Readers—for Ages 3 to 6
Picture Readers have super-simple texts, with many nouns appearing as rebus pictures. At the end of each book are 24 flash cards—on one side is the rebus picture; on the other side is the written-out word.

### Level 1—for Preschool through First-Grade Children
Level 1 books have very few lines per page, very large type, easy words, lots of repetition, and pictures with visual "cues" to help children figure out the words on the page.

### Level 2—for First-Grade to Third-Grade Children
Level 2 books are printed in slightly smaller type than Level 1 books. The stories are more complex, but there is still lots of repetition in the text, and many pictures. The sentences are quite simple and are broken up into short lines to make reading easier.

### Level 3—for Second-Grade through Third-Grade Children
Level 3 books have considerably longer texts, harder words, and more complicated sentences.

All Aboard for happy reading!

BT LE SG NC JR

*Library of Congress Cataloging-in-Publication Data*

Driscoll, Laura.
    Sammy Sosa—he's the man / by Laura Driscoll ; illustrated by Ken Call.
    p. cm. — (All aboard reading. Level 3)
    Summary: Presents the life and baseball career of Sammy Sosa, who, along with Mark McGwire, in 1998 broke the long-standing record of most home runs hit in a season.
    1. Sosa, Sammy, 1968- —Juvenile literature. 2. Baseball players—United States—Biography—Juvenile literature. Dominican (Dominican Republic)—Biography—Juvenile literature. [1. Sosa, Sammy, 1968- . 2. Baseball players. 3.Dominicans (Dominican Republic)—Biography.] I. Call. Ken, ill. II. Title. III. Series.
GV865.S59S68 1999
796.357'092—dc21                                                                    99-13641
[B]                                                                                              CIP

ISBN  0-448-42069-4  (GB)     A B C D E F G H I J
ISBN  0-448-42067-8 (pbk.)     A B C D E F G H I J

ALL
ABOARD
READING™

Level 3
Grades 2-3

# Sammy Sosa
## HE'S THE MAN

By Laura Driscoll
Illustrated by Ken Call

With photographs

Grosset & Dunlap • New York

J796.357
DRI

# Man of the Month

**June 25, 1998**
**Tiger Stadium, Detroit**

It is the top of the seventh inning. The Chicago Cubs are trailing the Detroit Tigers by a score of 3 to 1. The next batter is a six-foot-tall, 200-pound right fielder. He is a Cub. And yet, the Tigers' home crowd starts cheering the minute he steps up to the plate. Why is everyone so excited?

It's because this batter is not just any
Cub. He is number 21, Sammy Sosa,
Chicago's power slugger. All through
June, his bat has been on fire. And
baseball fans—no matter what team they
root for—love to watch Sammy in action.

Sosa began the month with home runs in five straight games. And now he has hit an amazing 18 home runs in June alone. He has already tied the major-league record for most home runs in a month— a record set more than sixty years ago.

Now, as Sosa steps up to the plate, Tiger fans watch and wait. Will the record be broken right now, right here in Tiger Stadium?

On the second pitch, the crowd gets its answer. Tiger pitcher Brian Moehler puts the ball over the plate. Sosa swings. *Crack!* Right away, Sosa knows it is a home run. He leaps into the air and watches as the ball sails over the right-field wall.

Sosa rounds the bases. Again, the crowd cheers wildly. Baseball fans love to see power sluggers hit balls out of the park. But with Sammy Sosa, it's more than that. People enjoy watching him play ball because he knows how to have fun. He always seems to be laughing or smiling. And he loves the crowd. At the start of each game in Chicago, Sosa puts his hand to his ear as he runs out to right field. It's his way of asking his home crowd to make some noise. And they do—every time.

Sosa is not the only one making baseball so exciting to watch in 1998. Mark McGwire of the St. Louis Cardinals is also racking up the home runs. By the middle of the summer, McGwire and Sosa are battling it out in the greatest race of them all—the race for most home runs in a season.

People who aren't even sports fans
start watching games. In fact, baseball
hasn't been so popular since before
the strike of 1994. Fans are flocking to
the ballparks. And together, Sosa and
McGwire are treating them to a season
they will never forget.

But for Sosa, this miracle season is just icing on the cake. He feels lucky just to be in the United States playing the game he loves. That alone is a childhood dream come true.

# Little Sammy

Sammy Sosa was born on November 12, 1968. He grew up in a town called San Pedro de Macorís in the Dominican Republic—a small country on a Caribbean island.

The Sosa family was poor. So little Sammy and his brothers helped out. They worked as shoeshine boys. They sold oranges. They washed cars. They did everything they could to earn money for the family.

That didn't leave Sammy very much time for playing baseball. But like a lot of Dominican kids, he loved the game. Many of the Dominican players in the major leagues were from Sammy's hometown. He and his friends dreamed of growing up to be just like them.

Whenever Sammy could, he played "street ball." He played with his friends in the muddy unpaved roads of town. They could not afford real baseball gloves or real baseballs. So they used a rolled-up sock for a ball. And they made gloves out of milk cartons or old pieces of canvas.

Then, when Sammy was fourteen, his mother let him join a baseball league. No more rolled-up socks or milk-carton mitts. Now he was playing with real equipment on a real baseball field, with uniforms and coaches. Sammy began to show those coaches what a great player he was.

American baseball scouts were in the Dominican Republic. They were looking for good young players to play for pro teams in the United States. And they found Sammy Sosa. In fact, scouts from many different teams wanted him. When Sammy was sixteen, he made his choice. He signed a contract to play in the minor leagues for the Texas Rangers.

Just a few years before, Sammy had been playing baseball on the street. Now he was going to the United States! He was going to be a pro baseball player! Could it be true? Sammy was still so young. But even then, Sosa was ready. Years later he said, "I did not care who I signed with. I only cared about signing and playing."

Now Sammy was going to get his chance.

# Slugger-in-Training

Sammy became a pro ball player quickly and easily. And he was making a name for himself in the minor leagues. Next, he set his sights on becoming a major-leaguer. That wasn't going to be easy. There were lots of other great players in the minor leagues. But after three strong years in the minors, Sammy got noticed. In 1989, he was traded to the Chicago White Sox and soon was playing for their major-league team! Now he, Sammy Sosa, was one of those Dominican major-leaguers he had looked up to as a kid!

Sammy played a good first year with the Sox. But then all of a sudden, in 1991, things got harder. Sosa had trouble with his hitting. His batting average was only .203 in 116 games. Was he just in a slump? Or had the Sox made a mistake with Sosa? The team didn't wait to find out. They traded Sosa across town to their rivals, the Chicago Cubs.

At first, the Cubs weren't so sure about Sosa either. He could not play for most of the '92 season because of a broken hand and a broken ankle. But in 1993, Sosa really started to prove himself. He hit 33 home runs and stole 36 bases! Sosa had made team history. He was the first Cub ever to hit more than 30 home runs and steal more than 30 bases in the same season.

In 1995, he hit 36 home runs. And the next year, he hit 40 home runs before an injury cut his season short.

As a hitter, Sosa had quick hands and a strong lower body that gave power to his swing. But some said that Sosa wasn't a smart hitter. Too often he would swing at bad pitches. And sometimes he seemed too eager to make a big hit. "I was trying to hit two home runs in every at bat," Sammy joked.

The Cubs' hitting coaches helped Sosa. He started standing farther from the plate. He kept his hands down. He shortened his swing. All of this gave Sosa more time to see each pitch. Sosa also worked on the timing of his swing. Finally, he learned how to be patient and wait for a good pitch.

Sosa was becoming a better all-around hitter. His hard work was paying off. But no one would know how much until the 1998 baseball season rolled around.

# The Home-Run Race of '98

By July of 1998, baseball fans everywhere had home-run fever. The record for most homers in one season had stood since 1961. That was when New York Yankee Roger Maris hit 61 homers. In all the years since then, only a couple of players had even come close to that magic number. But now, several players seemed to have a chance to pass it.

Early on in the '98 season, most of
the home-run headlines were about Mark
McGwire and Ken Griffey, Jr. McGwire
had homered 58 times in 1997. He was
big and strong. He hit high, towering
shots out of the park. Some of them
had flown over 500 feet. Many thought
he was the most likely to break Maris's
record.

Mark
McGwire

Ken Griffey, Jr.

Ken Griffey, Jr., of the Seattle Mariners had homered 56 times in 1997. And except for 1995 when he broke his wrist, he had hit 40 or more homers in every season since 1993. Now, in his tenth year in the major leagues, Griffey was a very smart, mature batter. Many people expected that he would also challenge the record.

But what about Sosa? At first, hardly anyone thought he would make a run at the record. Then, after Sosa hit so many home runs in June, people were keeping an eye on him too. Sosa became known for his line-drive homers, his good humor, and for blowing kisses. After each home run, Sosa touched his heart to say thank you to the fans. Then he blew a kiss. It was for his mother back home in the Dominican Republic.

By the end of July, Sosa had blown a lot of kisses. He had 42 homers—one more than Griffey and only three behind McGwire. And by mid-August, the home-run race had become a battle of the bats between Sosa and McGwire.

On August 19, Sosa hit home run number 48. The same day, McGwire hit his 48th and 49th homers—both in one game. From that point on, the race was neck and neck.

Every day, newspapers and sports shows covered the story of "Slammin' Sammy" and "Big Mac." Reporters spoke to Sosa and McGwire together. The two players laughed and joked with each other. They played for different teams, but they were good sports. And they were becoming good friends too. Sosa said that

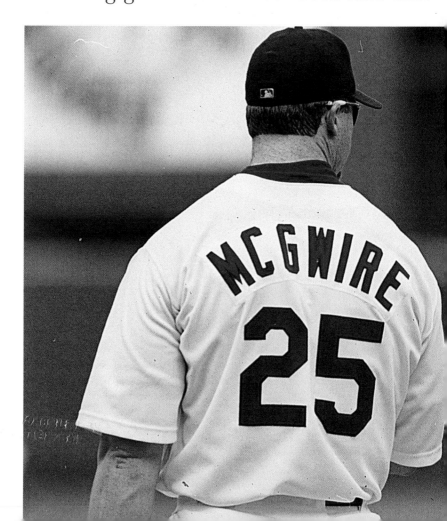

he looked up to McGwire, almost the way a son looks up to his father. "To me, just being behind Mark McGwire is being a winner. I'm no Mark McGwire. He's the man," said Sosa. He made everyone like him even more by being so humble. He thought McGwire would probably be the first to break Maris's record.

Then on September 8, it happened. In a Cubs-Cardinals game in St. Louis, McGwire hit number 62. Sosa was there to see it. After McGwire had rounded the bases, Sosa jogged in from the outfield. He hugged McGwire and yelled, "You did it!"

Sosa hugs McGwire after his 62nd home run.

Days later, Sosa reached the same mark. On September 13, Sosa hit his 61st and 62nd homers in the same game. It was a home game at Wrigley Field against the Milwaukee Brewers. More than 40,000 people packed the stadium. They took pictures and waved Dominican flags in honor of Sammy. Meanwhile, outside the ballpark, people fought over the two home-run balls.

Afterwards, McGwire said, "People have been saying for thirty-seven years that this couldn't be done, and yet two guys have done it."

And the season wasn't over yet! Now the question was: Who would have the most home runs at the end of the season?

But Sosa had other things to think about besides the home-run race.

The Chicago Cubs had a shot at making the playoffs. But it was going to be close. More than ever, Sosa had to focus on winning games, not on hitting home runs. And Sosa was ready to bunt or take a walk if it would help his team. He put the team first. "Making the playoffs is more important than hitting home runs," Sammy said to reporters.

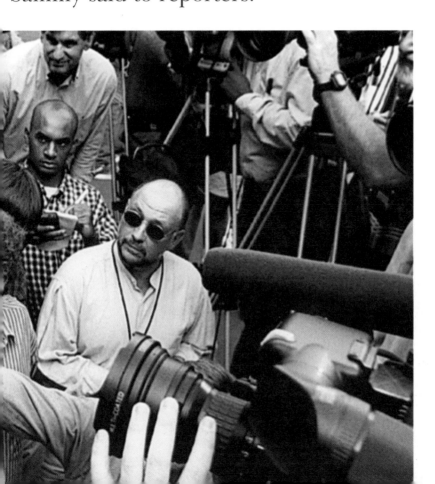

By the last weekend of the season, Sosa and McGwire were tied at 65 homers. On Friday, September 25, Sosa hit homer number 66 in the Houston Astrodome. So did McGwire in St. Louis. The race was going right down to the wire. Each player had only two more games left to play. Would they end up tying for the record? Both Sosa and McGwire said if that happened, it would be great.

But it didn't. In his last two games, McGwire went homer happy. He hit two home runs in each game. That gave him a grand total of 70. Sosa stayed at 66. So McGwire was the new home-run king.

Still, Sammy had so much to be happy about. The season had been the best of his career. And his power hitting had gotten him something he wanted even more than a home-run title. Sosa's team was going to the playoffs. It was the first time the Chicago Cubs had made it to the postseason since 1989.

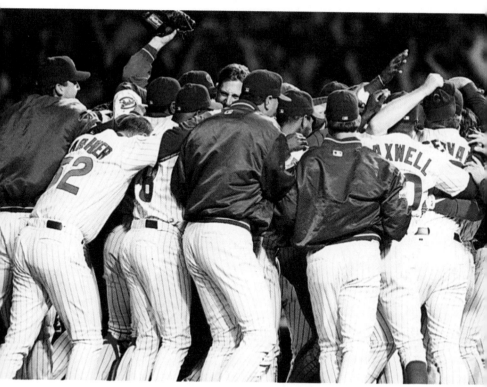

The Chicago Cubs celebrate after winning a spot in the playoffs.

The Cubs couldn't have done it without
Sammy's bat. Twenty-one of Sosa's home
runs had given the Cubs the lead in the
game. Six had tied the game. Sosa had
also helped the team as a great all-around
hitter. He finished with more RBIs and
more runs scored than any other player
in 1998.

Because of these stats, Sammy Sosa was named the National League's Most Valuable Player for 1998. Sosa got 30 first-place votes while McGwire got two. McGwire had hit more home runs. But many people thought Sosa had done more to help his team.

## International Hero

The 1998 season made Sammy Sosa
a baseball legend not only in the United
States, but around the world. In the
Dominican Republic and other Latino
countries, he had already been well
known for years. But after hitting 66
home runs, Sosa joined the ranks of the
greatest Latino sports heroes of all time.

Sammy Sosa had come a long way. But he did not forget where he came from. Whenever he could, Sosa gave back to the people of San Pedro. He bought new computers for the schools and more ambulances for the town. He built stores and office buildings, and opened the Sammy Sosa Baseball School. For Christmas 1997, Sosa went to San Pedro as "Sammy Claus." He gave out presents to children in schools and hospitals. And when Hurricane Georges hit the Dominican Republic in 1998, Sosa was quick to help out. He traveled around the world, raising money to rebuild his country.

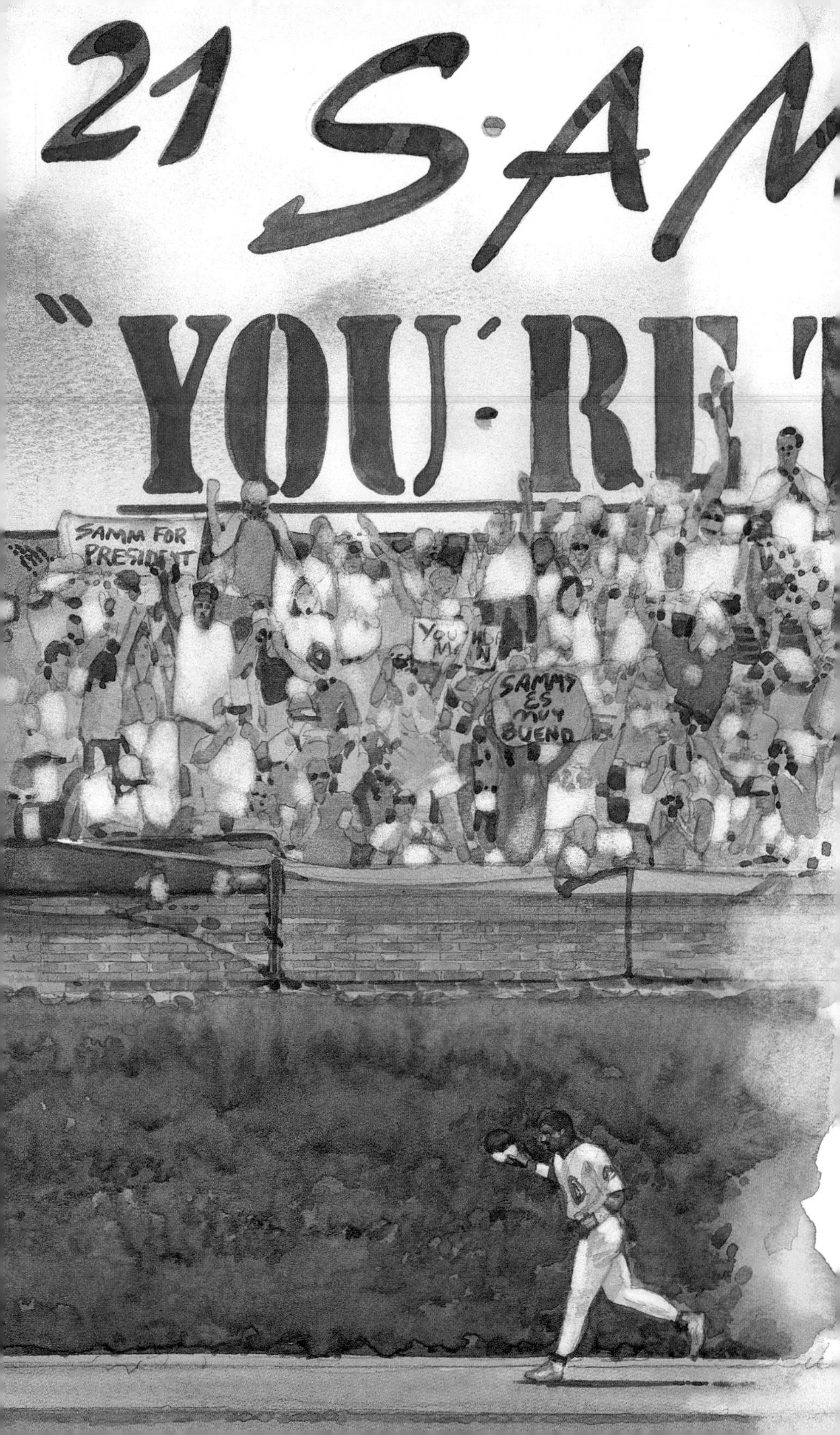
21 SAM
"YOU'RE
SAMM FOR
PRESIDENT
SAMMY
ES
MUY
BUENO

After the '98 season was over, Sosa was honored as a sports hero around the United States. In Chicago, thousands of fans turned out for a Sammy Sosa Celebration at Wrigley Field. They held signs that said "Sammy Sosa, You're the Man" and "Sosa for President."

In New York City, Sosa was given a big parade through a street called the "Canyon of Heroes." It got the name because parades on that street are usually just for astronauts, war heroes,

and presidents. Then the mayor of New York gave Sosa a key to the city. He called Sammy "a Dominican hero, an American hero, a hero around the world."

As for Sammy, he said he would rather be remembered for his deeds off the field. "I'd rather have people remember me one day for being a good person first, and a good ballplayer second," he said. But the world won't have to choose one or the other. People will remember Sammy Sosa as both. He is the man!